I0575452

DRAGONS N' ANTIBODIES

Linh Nguyen-Ng

Dragons N' Antibodies
Text copyright © 2020 by Linh Nguyen-Ng
Cover Design copyright © 2020 by Linh Nguyen-Ng

All rights reserved. Published by Prose & Concepts LLC.

No part of this book may be reproduced or transmitted
in any form or by any means, electronic, or mechanical,
including photocopying, recording, or by any information
storage and retrieval system without written permission
from the publisher. For information:

Prose & Concepts LLC
210 Park Avenue, Suite #280
Worcester, MA 01609
www.proseandconcepts.com

This book is a work of fiction. All characters, places, names,
and events are a product of the author's imagination.
Any resemblance to events, locations, or persons alive or
otherwise, is entirely coincidental.

Library of Congress Cataloging-in-Publication Data
Library of Congress Control Number: 2020932961
First edition Paperback ISBN: 978-1-7323275-6-6
First edition Ebook ISBN: 978-1-7323275-7-3

PROSE & CONCEPTS

I dedicate this book to the human body, its cells, and DNA. They are the reasons why we get to experience this sacred life here on Earth.

The only way to discover the limits of the possible is to go beyond them into the impossible.

— Arthur C. Clarke

As a scientist, Nathan Wu engaged in dialogue mainly with logic and facts. As the father of an extremely sick child, he found himself conversing with the illogical and believing in the unfathomable. And at times, wishing for the impossible.

Desperation often pushed people to the edge. He and his wife, Heather, were desperate to find a cure for their fourteen-year-old daughter, Rena. Despite her severe condition, she remained strong, persistent, and positive.

I've got this, Daddy. Rena's voice echoed in his head.

Her words, ambition, and tenacity were his constant reminders and the reasons he was still working in his laboratory at eleven at night long after his wife had gone home to their daughter. He could see Heather playing several games of Scrabble with Rena before the medication pushed her into a deep sleep.

Sitting at his desk, Nathan stared into his

electron microscope. His heart sank at the image of the virus attacking her dying white blood cells. "No," he said and switched to a new Petri dish.

His heart shattered as he watched her cells succumb to the unknown disease inside her once again. The new medication he and his wife spent months formulating had failed. "No, no, no!" Gripping his head, he stepped back from the microscope, scrubbing his face as if the action would remove his frustration.

You're looking at it all wrong. The voice in his head started again, sounding more urgent.

Nathan told himself exhaustion was the reason behind the recurring voices. But fatigue wasn't the only thing playing him like a drug. Disappointment, irritation, and hopelessness all glared at him like a sick specimen under examination.

Look at the unconventional. A voice that was neither male nor female spoke calmly.

Be less academic. This voice had a higher pitch.

Your intuition knows everything. The echo to this voice reminded him of something from outer space.

"LEAVE ME ALONE!" He snarled at the absurd and inexplicable dialogue that kept inserting itself into his head.

An image of two spirals flashed before him. He blinked, and they disappeared. This wasn't the first time he'd seen them. Strange voices and odd images had been hounding him for days, slowing down his progress.

Because it was getting late, he pushed the annoyance away. He should head home now if he wanted to be presentable and coherent for tomorrow morning's conference, where his coworker,

Lisa Matthews, would reveal new discoveries from her travels.

Inhaling a deep breath to clear his mind, he returned to the microscope, hoping to see some positive news. What he saw depressed him even more. The virus had mutated, becoming twice its size. It had been helical in shape, reminding him of a rigatoni pasta tube. Now it had morphed into a sphere, or specifically, an icosahedral. He blinked, and saw long tentacles extend from this strange virus, attacking Rena's cells and breaking down the membranes swiftly. Then the virus multiplied itself within the host cells. Fear squeezed Nathan's heart, making his chest ache.

A few more blinks, and he found himself staring at an army of mutant viruses he had never seen before. His vision blurred and he thought he saw eyes on them. He shook his head clear, rubbed his eyes with the heels of palms, and squinted into the microscope. The eyes had disappeared, but the sphere-shaped viruses were still there, destroying Rena's bodily defense system at an alarming rate.

"The answers you're looking for aren't there. Look beyond science, Nathan."

The sudden sound of a voice right next to him startled him out of his chair, knocking over his cup of engineered blue coffee. The one designed to be more effective than regular caffeine. It obviously didn't work because he was discombobulated, which would explain this madness.

"Who's there?" He glanced around the lab while reaching for the roll of paper towel on the opposite side of the counter.

He didn't see anyone. No one would be visiting his personal lab this late in the night. The fluorescent light appeared dimmer than usual, making him feel drowsy. The heaviness on his eyelids and the silence in the room didn't help his concentration. In fact, he felt lopsided like a tree that would fall at the slightest push. His sensory neurons felt like they were already tucked in bed, not allowing him full access to his senses.

Exhaling an exhausted huff, he cursed as he wiped the coffee spill from the files, including the notebook where he had documented every hypothesis, formula, and diagram of Rena's medical treatments. He didn't have time for delays, obstacles, or mayhem.

Frustration flared. "What do you want from me? Who are you?"

"We are you." There was a familiarity to this voice that was now clear, but he couldn't decipher where he had heard it before. "You asked us for help. We're here to help."

A swirl of colorful light spun out from the space in front of him, reminding him of a nebula from the sky. Chills raced down his spine as he grabbed a pair of dirty scissors from a nearby tool tray, preparing for the unexpected. Preparing to defend himself.

Where was this swirl coming from? Moreover, *what* was coming out of it? His heart thundered, screaming at him to wake up from whatever dream this was. He backed away from the energy swirl and a sharp pain punctured his rib cage. His hand flew to the injured area. He glanced down and found blood smeared across his skin. Blood caused by the uncleansed scalpel he'd left on the counter. *Shit.* What had he used that on? He couldn't remember. Fear had blocked everything out.

His heart rate escalated. Revelation pierced through him. *This is no dream.*

4

Nathan tried to remember who he had asked for help. The past year had been difficult. Rena's allergic reaction to engineered foods reached a point where dangerous symptoms flared up even with organic food. So he had prayed to God, to the angels, and to his ancestors to protect his child. Damn it, he had prayed to anyone and anything that could help her.

Was God spiraling before him? His gut told him no. God would be more direct and had more important things to do than spook a scientist. Could this be an angel with a strange sense of humor? Or one of his ancestors? The voice did sound familiar, but he couldn't place it.

As if the swirl understood his questions, the spinning slowed as the voice spoke, "We're your DNA."

His DNA?

The bizarre idea birthed a laugh that wanted to come out, but fear trapped it in his throat.

His curiosity replied before his rational mind could stop it. "What do you mean?" He gripped the scissors tighter and wondered who or what was speaking from the glowing swirl of energy. It had grown to the same size as his own body. "I only hear one of you."

Instantly, he felt a rush a warm energy bloom on the crown of his head, cascading over his face, down his neck, arms, shoulders, stomach, and legs. Each sensation woke something inside him, making him more aware of his body and his surroundings. What he saw next astonished him.

Transfixed him.

In the center of the colorful swirl, two spiraling strands of energy emerged. They entered the room like two iridescent snakes that soon took on the appearance of abstract dragons. As they spiraled around each other, he recognized the image they created: the double helix!

The two strands multiplied and became four, then six, then eight, and eventually stopped at twelve. All the iridescent strands—no, dragons— wove around each other, blending with one another as they took on geometric shapes. When the strands formed his face, he let out a loud gasp and dropped the scissors. They clanked somewhere under the counter. He didn't dare take his eyes off of the spirals before him and acknowledge he was weaponless. Not that the germ-infested scissors would do anything against this strange abnormality.

"We are you." The voice bounced around the lab, creating a syncopated rhythm. "You're looking at your own DNA. Every strand is a part of you. We heard your desperation."

Nathan stood motionless, speechless. What could he possibly say to his DNA? *"Hey, how are you doing?"* or *"Why do you look like dragons?"* didn't sound normal.

At the moment, nothing could sound normal. The thought of having a conversation with something he had studied under a microscope blew his mind. He examined the energetic face, contemplating how his DNA could be talking to him like this. Like it had its own mind, its own consciousness, its own being.

Was it possible that in his desperation to heal Rena he'd called out to some magical world? He had read enough science fiction and fantasy books to know that such fantastical things only existed in books or movies.

Logic spiraled to the forefront of his mind

and begged for proof. Was he the first person to experience this kind of crazy dialogue with DNA? Had this happened before and the phenomenon was kept secret? He'd definitely look into it later.

The multi-strands detangled their formation of his face and fused into two long dragons. "Come with us. We'll show you how you can help your daughter. The potential of humanity is on the other side of the veil."

In that instant he recognized the familiarity of the voice. It was his own voice slightly skewed as if it had been synthesized. More than anything, this voice extracted something deep from within him, illuminating moments in his life that he had forgotten, from his childhood, his chaotic teen years, and all the struggles and accomplishments of his adult life. And something more that he couldn't quite grasp.

Then an image popped to the front of Nathan's mind. It was the day he had taught his fearless seven-year-old Rena how to ride a bicycle. It only took her one afternoon to master the task. The following day, confidence beamed on her face as she rode the bike around the neighborhood not once, but twice. She didn't let her fragile health get in her way.

"You could learn from her," the dragons said, fanning out their long tails like peacock feathers.

He didn't know if that revelation scared him more than if the voice had been that of a stranger. He found himself in a perplexed state. Unlike his scientific self that always followed a detailed plan and *knew* what to do next, but in his current state of mind, Nathan was acknowledging an intuition, the one that had helped him guide his daughter during her bike lesson.

Something spiked in him as he stared at the iridescent strands that transformed into visible serpentine dragons with scales, eyes, and wings. The dragons swayed back and forth in the air as they considered him.

Fear and nerves bubbled in his stomach. Where was this place they wanted him to see? Could Rena's cure be there?

"Let the fear go. Trust us. Trust yourself." The swirl pulsed, sending out sparkles of gold that twinkled like stars. "Come see something that hasn't been shown to a human before."

This energy cut through the muck of his mind and he knew he wanted to find out what was beyond that vortex. The scientist in him was curious. Moreover, the father in him wanted to give Rena every opportunity to live a happy life. She deserved it.

Somehow, a calmness grew as the two DNA-dragons swam around him. His muscles relaxed, his breathing slowed, and the fear that had him hesitating at first disappeared.

So many questions crowded his mind, but he focused on the practical ones. Where would this portal take him? Would he meet strange creatures like the ones he read in books? The boy in him also wondered if he'd gain some magical skill. Would he return the same person? Would he return at all or be stuck in some dimension where his wife and daughter could never find him?

"Do not fear, you'll return to your family," said the voice.

There was a truth—an integrity—to this voice that seeped into his bones. He could trust it.

Inhaling a deep breath to ground himself, Nathan stepped closer to the brightness at the center of the vortex. The two dragons spun on either side as if holding up the energetic curtains. He expected the strong force to suck him in, but only a gentle breeze brushed his face and hair. Under his feet were gold stones that shifted shapes.

He stepped on a round stone, and the curtains of light drew close. Right away, a new pair of curtains opened, revealing a Universe where colorful nebulas and star clusters emerged before him like actors on a cosmic stage. Circles of lights danced across the sky like soap bubbles. The colors flowed like watercolor, blending into each other. The stars appeared as if an artist just dotted them in front of him.

He moved onto another stone, and discovered that his equilibrium was fine. The vibrancy of colors and stars increased as if his eyes had special lenses that modified themselves to the phenomenon. He inhaled, and the abundance of oxygen invigorated his body. All around him, particles flowed and created this lovely chatter as if they spoke to each other in a secret language. Some geometric shapes floated and connected to each other like puzzle pieces.

What magical world was this?

Above him, a swarm of centipede-like things skimmed the top of his head with their long legs. One insect glanced at him with its four eyes before crawling into a swirling black hole, interrupted by twinkling stars laced within the nebulas. About twenty feet away, the same insect emerged from a new black swirl, continuing its entrance and exit through the vortices.

Nathan scanned the area and studied the ground beyond the stones. In the distance was blackness, but closer up he couldn't tell if it was soil, rocks, or grass. A layer of thick fog covered everything. The vapors ascended and descended as if someone was breathing in and out. He wondered what would happen if he stepped off the path. Would he fall into an abyss, or would it be solid ground?

He didn't have time to contemplate, before a mob of white balls rolled past him, chasing some red discs. They created this delightful sound that resembled children's laughter. Puddles of liquids splashed from the playful match. The liquids squirted into his face. He winced, using the back of his hand to wipe it clean. One white ball that looked like a munchkin donut hole flew before his eyes, allowing him to see details of it.

Then realization blasted into him.

Holy shit. His heart galloped with excitement at what he was seeing. Of what he was experiencing. He'd been too bewildered by the entirety of everything that he didn't make the connection sooner.

"HOLY SHIT," he said aloud, watching the giant white blood cells playing with the red ones. They looked like white munchkins playing with interesting red buttons. These things were twice his size, even though he had been looking at them all day through the microscope. The texture on the white blood cells now in their huge form appeared like unique architecture. And the red blood cells resembled huge buttons roaming around like flying saucers. He recognized them despite their distortions.

The sounds they made had rhythm and tonality that added purpose and power to what he was witnessing. Before this moment, he would have dismissed the absurd notion immediately.

But now, he found himself entertaining it.

This reality of encountering a fantastical version of human biology was mind-blowing. The same amazement was applied to his ability to communicate with his own DNA like friends chatting over coffee.

Fifty feet away, something moved on a wall of pulsating energy. As he approached, he saw wriggling blobs and nightmarish creatures encapsulated inside the energetic wall like prisoners. Scratching the wall, they reached for him with their claws and tails, but the energy prevented them from going beyond a few inches from their prison.

The hair on his neck rose from the sight and eerie snarls. What were these beings, and why were they trapped? He noticed several white blood cells with golden auras hovering around this cage as if they were guarding them.

His mind went into explorative mode. These terrifying creatures could be viruses and bacteria. He was seeing what diseases looked like inside the human body.

That idea intrigued, baffled, and scared him. A loud noise rumbled like an earthquake. The stones under his feet flared red and began to shake. The nebulas and star clusters that had given light to his surroundings dulled, turning the environment dark and spooky.

Right away, four strands in red, blue, yellow, and green appeared beside him, twisting and twirling. "Enjoy the show," the red strand said.

"Pay attention." The blue strand spun around the red one.

The yellow spiraled close to his face. "Details matter."

"Look beyond the science," said the green

one as it fused itself to its comrades and vanished.

Nathan noted some stars and nebulas remained vibrant, but they were in a constant flux between brightness and dullness as if low on power.

The noise grew louder from behind him, and he whirled, facing a monstrous grey ball about three times his size with two eyes and multiple tentacles. It glared at him from twenty feet away.

The tentacles reached for him, allowing him to see the geometric shapes at their ends. Some appeared like a key that would fit into something; others looked like a socket for something to go into. Though there was nothing angelic about this creature, a yellow halo surrounded the sphere, creating its own light. What an oxymoron the image made: a haloed monster. Its surface undulated as if fluids were trying to push their way out.

Gurgling noises erupted from the creature as a toxic smell attacked Nathan's nose, churning his stomach. His heart raced as he tried to find a way to escape. The darkness around him made it difficult to see anything besides the stone path. But he had to risk it.

He stepped off the path and his feet landed on a spongy surface. The surface glowed softly, giving him an idea of what he stood on. He could see about two feet ahead, but no more. The surface wobbled and gave a slight bounce with each movement like he was on a trampoline.

Nathan bounded away from the creature as doubts bloomed in his mind. Had he made a mistake by entering this portal? Was everything a trick just to get him here so this monster could devour him? Where did his DNA go? Was the DNA just an illusion? Had he unknowingly poisoned himself with something in the lab that was causing him to hallucinate? A heartbeat later, he remembered the dirty scalpel that had punctured his skin. He'd used it on several rat specimens infested with the cold and flu viruses.

His mind was still on the stupid scalpel when he tumbled from an unexpected dip in the spongy ground, throwing him into a thorny bush. A curse exploded from his mouth at the same time that heat exploded in his bicep. A thorn had pierced his shirt, ripping it open and taking a piece of his flesh with it. Blood and pain erupted, verifying the fact that he was in real danger here.

He needed to get back home to his family.

The beast laughed. "You're on *my* turf." It growled like a starving dog. "You must die." Its wide mouth was like a cave that expanded over half of its mass. For a moment, Nathan wondered if that dark mass was another portal into another terrifying world.

Panic rose in him; he knew he could become this creature's snack. He wished he had never entered this portal, never trusted his DNA.

He glanced around. The atmosphere now resembled a massive bruise with cloud clusters of dark burgundy, purples, and shades of black. With the use of its many tentacles, the beast approached him. Instinct pushed Nathan's feet back. He wanted to run fast, but something slowed his reaction. The idleness allowed him to see the creature in more detail.

As the grey monster moved, gel-like things seeped from its pores. The gel shifted and grew into smaller replicas of the monster. The way the replication took place and the way the "halo" appeared on each smaller being took Nathan's breath away.

Revelation chilled him. He was looking at the coronavirus and its replicas. The coronaviruses were known to cause the common cold. The same viruses he had been experimenting on with his cutting-edge medications. The viruses have a halo appearance when viewed under an electron microscope. It was easier to see the familiar features with the smaller versions.

So many studies to destroy this group of viruses had failed. Nathan knew the coronavirus was an RNA virus, which meant it could skip a step when it replicated itself, as opposed to a DNA virus that had to transcribe into RNA first. A gut feeling told him there was something in this detail that would be useful to him, but he didn't have time to ponder it.

Right now, his mind was focused on survival. What if this monstrous virus wasn't trying to devour him? What if this coronavirus carried another horrible disease that it wanted him to spread? He'd rather die here than bring something back to his family.

Nathan didn't have time to further contemplate before the giant coronavirus propelled toward him like a beastly lawn mower with the help of its tentacles. It wobbled from side to side, rushing toward him.

He fled, springing from the spongy ground. The strange hold that had slowed him down earlier disappeared under his adrenaline rush, fear, or something else. He didn't know which, and he didn't care.

Glancing back, he saw the smaller coronas following suit. The squishing ground didn't delay them, for their tentacles extended out as anchors. His feet quickened, but halted when he saw three pathways. Where would these lead?

Several flashes caught his eye in the distance,

but his attention went to the blooming heat and pain in his bicep and the injury on his rib cage. Turning right on the closest path, he saw something flash, illuminating the nearby area. A strange thing occurred. The flashes coincided with his throbbing heat and pain. He'd make the connection later.

He darted into a forest, where the trees looked like broccoli and strange plant succulents, hoping they would obscure him. From behind a bush, he watched the small coronaviruses speed past him, whipping their tentacles around.

Relief settled for a moment as flashes illuminated the darkness like lightning. Then something emerged from those flashes, but they were too far in the distance for him to see clearly.

Suddenly, he felt a pinch on his right ankle. A breath later, a chill climbed up his leg, cramping his muscles. He glanced down and found an oblong creature that resembled a horrendous grub the size of a giant turkey grinder standing inches from him. It had a sharp tail and three eyes that glared at him the way cancer would glare at its antidote. The look it gave him was more vicious than that of the coronavirus. He didn't even know where that thought about cancer had come from.

Details matter. The DNA words echoed in his head. Were these clues for him?

That theory and everything else vanished from his mind when a fever erupted inside him. Simultaneously, yellow light burst in the air in front of him like fireworks. Next, a vein-like web spread across the sky like inflamed lightning. It pulsed, sending out a wave of heat that he felt on his skin. He felt the echo of that blaze inside of him.

He found himself struggling to breathe as the muscles inside his chest tightened. A noise that sounded like static crackled beside him. The fog that had covered the ground began to subside, and bubbles of light floated around in conjunction with the flaming, veined lightning, allowing him to see clearly. The bumpy ground heaved like it was a diaphragm, rising and falling in the same way he was struggling for breath.

"What in God's name?" he gasped as the epiphany blasted through his barrier of scientific logic. Comprehension overcame him. *He was inside his own body.* He was witnessing the action and reaction of what was happening internally being reflected to his external environment.

The creature jumped onto his leg, crawling up and up. Clutching his chest, Nathan swatted it down and kicked it away. It snarled and scurried back toward him. With a cramped leg, he stumbled from his hideout, revealing himself to the coronaviruses. But they weren't alone now. An army of geometric beings emerged from several yellow bursts in the air, surrounded the viruses, and neutralized them. More flashes illuminated the area as more pain ruptured inside him.

How could he explain that he had teleported into a fantastical world of his own body? Who would believe him? Would his wife, Heather, believe him? How could he prove that he was looking at versions of antibodies, the police force of the immune system, this close?

This *animated.*

What he saw defied everything he'd ever learned.

Holy God, before him were white blood cells, phagocytes, lymphocytes all performing their roles as defenders of their home. It was as if each being had its own consciousness and knew exactly what

16

to do. Here in this space, they were beings living their lives, and he was the foreign agent.

The light bursts he had seen earlier were the activation of the defensive response. The mastery of what he was seeing—of what he was discerning—astounded him. His body shuddered as if agreeing with him. The shudder brought him back to the pain in his leg and rib cage, the heat on his bicep, the tightening in his chest, and cautioned him about the source of these symptoms.

He turned toward the grub that was now being torn apart by the Y-shaped antibodies. The battle sounded and smelled like a garbage disposal breaking food apart. He took the opportunity to flee somewhere safe. However, his weakened body didn't allow for rushed movement.

Out of nowhere, something clutched at his feet, whipped him around so he was flat on his back. The distorted thing dragged him into a secluded area where darkness was the landscape. Bubbles of light hovered beside him, illuminating the horror.

His heart lurched at the sight of a morphed coronavirus with its spiky tentacles clasping his feet. This creature was twice the size of the giant one that had chased him earlier. This beast had several mouths, tongues, and appendages, including small insects that flickered red heat as they moved around on the monster's body.

Nathan screamed when the heat from its tentacles burned through his khakis and socks, penetrating his skin. The entire sky flared neon red, reflecting his heat and pain. The venom singed his blood to the point where he felt it bubble, oozing out of him. The pain from this mutant coronavirus was a hundred times worse than that of the cancerous grub. He felt his bodily systems collapse. Suddenly, the landscape and trees in front of him began to crumble and fall.

"Help me!" He shouted for his DNA. "Where the hell did you go?"

He didn't know how it was possible, but he could actually *feel* his cells reacting to this foreign attack. His vision blurred and when he blinked, images flashed before him.

On the ground, using a hand to balance, he *felt* and *saw* his cells fighting the intruders. Not only was he watching a live show of his own body being attacked, he was living it. He felt the communication between his internal cells and the ones in front of his eyes. He heard abstract sounds, but somehow he knew what they meant. Intuition shot into his heart and spoke to him. For the first time in his life, he understood the call, and it had nothing to do with logic. He took a deep breath and began his command.

"Fuse, mutate, regenerate, replicate," he said in a stern voice. "Heal me."

Think beyond science, echoed inside his head. Though pain stabbed him everywhere, the strong feeling in his gut rose to the top. "Work together to *benefit* me."

Immediately, a golden spark glowed inside his cells, the mutant coronavirus, and the cancerous grub, like an invisible communication that had been understood by all of them. The process reminded him of Christmas lights when every single bulb lit up from a switch. His body shuddered as if his words had activated an internal manual.

Nathan watched spirals of his DNA transcribing into RNA. Geometric symbols in various colors, soothing sounds, and clear fluids from the

18

DNA attached themselves to the RNA strand for the transfer of information. The RNA was now a messenger dragon, traveling to other organisms to convey the data. The RNA-dragons were shorter than the DNA ones.

Symbols, sounds, and fluids that exited from the RNA were seamlessly accepted and absorbed by the viruses and bacteria. He didn't see any hesitation or resistance and knew that the RNA was collaborating with the "enemies" in a way he never thought was possible.

Curiosity whipped his attention to the coronavirus and the cancerous grub. The golden spark still glowed at their centers as the RNA-dragons communicated with them. But this communication involved more intricate symbols and loud noises, making the coronavirus and the cancerous grub tremble. The two toxins rattled a unique language that burst out circular golden symbols and energetic sounds that made Nathan ponder what they were saying to each other. It also made him wonder on the possibility of playing poison with poison.

Right away, the ground and sky quaked, reflecting his body's reaction to the two poisons working together with his body to benefit him. Heat and ice ran from his head to his toes while red and blue lights shot back and forth in the sky like a beautiful light show. As the web of veins subsided to a soft pink glow like that of a lovely sunset, the crumbling landscape began to rebuild itself. Fallen trees straightened up, echoing his molecular structure transforming into something new.

Impossible.

Soon, the burning eased and the pain reduced dramatically, even though the coronavirus still had long tentacles wrapped around his legs.

Then the blue DNA strand glowed beside him. "You told them what to do. You told us what to do."

He did. His commands had worked. That relieved him, but it also shocked him at how easy it was.

"I begged for your help!" Anger injected into each word. "You didn't come. Where were you? Did you enjoy my suffering?"

Abruptly, the coronavirus loosened its grip and Nathan scooted away. He climbed to his feet.

The monster grew in size until it was monumental. It propelled toward him slowly with its multiple mouths growling. With all his strength, Nathan ran, but the beast was too fast. Six tentacles grabbed him, yanking him back into its massive mouth. It stank of rotting flesh. Bile rose in his throat as the abyss swallowed him.

Right away, silence and darkness cloaked him. The rhythm of his heartbeat slowed and his muscles relaxed. He walked around the darkness like he was at the center of the Universe with particles sparkling in the distance.

He stepped forward and was immediately transported back into his office. He didn't see any portal, only the twelve colorful strands of DNA-dragons glowing and spinning in front of him.

"You did well." The purple dragon slithered like a serpent through the air.

Anger rose in him as he remembered the agony. "You almost killed me!"

"But we didn't. It was the best way for you to experience the divinity of it. You wouldn't have believed us," said the blue-green strand. "We couldn't explain these things to you without you seeing and *feeling* them firsthand."

Divinity? He let out a short laugh that had the DNA-dragons stop spiraling as if he had offended them.

He didn't know if it was guilt or shame that had him sighing. It was true. If he hadn't experienced this event, he would not have believed it. "I saw my cellular structure *restructuring* in a way that science has never seen. My DNA decoded and recoded in a way that didn't make any sense. I saw my RNA communicating with diseased cells like fantasy-beings having a casual conversation." He shook his head in disbelief. "I saw and felt my biology transform at a subatomic level."

An idea sprouted in the corner of his mind, but he couldn't grasp it. However, he recognized the enthusiasm. This discovery, this out-of-this-world experience was the breakthrough he needed for his daughter, Rena.

"Your body understands the thoughts in your head." Two orange dragons whipped their long bodies around the lab like wheat in a field. "Your intention, your command, is powerful."

A glowing yellow dragon wove itself around a green one. "Intent changes everything." The two dragons became a single aqua dragon with long whiskers and diamond scales.

"What do you mean?" Nathan had a hunch, but he wanted to hear it from them.

"Communicate with your body. Talk to us. *Ask* us for help." All the dragons came together and created a beautiful geometric pattern that splashed across the room. "Think beyond the conventional. You're not linear just as we're not a two-stranded entity." The pattern formed a smile. "DNA is intelligent. Therefore, the body is intelligent. But this intelligence is quantum. It's multidimensional. You can alter and heal your body on an atomic level simply by directing us."

The marvel of talking to his DNA and learning from it was something he'd never tire of. If DNA was quantum, then it had to be true that humans were also quantum.

The dragons read his mind, nodded, and spiraled like they were celebrating.

This unconventional way of thinking didn't exist in science books. "It's difficult for me to accept this mystery, this...*wonder* of what you're telling me. What you're showing me."

"We know."

His mind was like a kid's bedroom, so cluttered with stuff he didn't know where to begin. One thing was clear: he had to test his blood in case he had inadvertently caught some strange disease while he was inside that other realm.

"There's no need to worry about your health. But go ahead and check." The green dragon glowed, sounding like it was daring him.

He had gone through the portal to retrieve information for his daughter's health, but if he wasn't alive to help her, then it was useless.

"How am I supposed to help my daughter?" Nathan glanced at his counter. Everything was as he had left it. His microscope, documents, and notebook hadn't moved an inch. "You showed me a mutant coronavirus and a nasty cancerous grub. What's the connection between them? What am I supposed to understand?"

"You have all the information you require. We can only meet you halfway." The red dragon glowed. "Think, but not in the linear fashion you're used to. Think in terms of quantum energy. A quantum state doesn't have a past, present, or future.

It's everywhere at the same time. Take gravity and magnetism; they are interdimensional forces. Both are invisible and unexplainable. Yet, they exist everywhere. The quantum is like that. It has many realities that occur simultaneously. Some things that don't normally make sense to you in 3D will make sense in a quantum state."

Nathan recalled his experience inside the human body. When he was there witnessing that miraculous world, everything made sense. That world existed in itself and it didn't need any explanation. But now, as he tried to analyze it, it confused him. There were too many questions.

Nonetheless, he didn't want to let his DNA know about his doubts. Maybe they already knew by reading his thoughts, but wanted him to figure them all out himself.

Nathan said, "Tonight has changed everything for me."

"That was the intention," they replied. "DNA is a portal into other worlds. Right now, in your reality, what you know about DNA is about 1% of what it truly is."

Nathan's eyebrows squished together as he imagined all the hard work from scientists around the world labeled as a mere "one percent."

If DNA was divine like it described itself, then it should know everything. "What disease does my daughter have?" Nathan asked. "Why can't you just tell me so I can heal her faster?"

The pattern made of dragons chuckled and shrank until it took on a sphere design that mimicked the Flower of Life. It was mesmerizing to watch. "It doesn't work that way. There's a learning process to everything. It's part of the human evolution."

"What if my experiments end up hurting her

even more?" An image of Rena suffering, crying out, begging for help, constricted his chest. "What if I end up killing her because I think *way* outside the box?"

"You won't," they said. "We know this because her DNA is part of us, too. She is the way she is because she is needed for the breakthrough that *you* will create. There's a plan within the plan."

Their statement infuriated him. "You're telling me Rena is sick by divine design?" His voice rose, but he couldn't help it. "That her pain and suffering was created on purpose?"

"We all serve a purpose to something, to someone, Nathan. There's a higher order to everything that you can't possibly understand right now. Don't be angry with the Universe. Look at this incident as an opportunity to make things better. Saving your daughter will save others as well."

A headache bloomed inside Nathan and he knew part of it was exhaustion and lack of sleep. A part of him heard them, but as a father, he couldn't fathom the thought that someone had placed his daughter in this dire situation just to teach him a lesson.

Automatically, images of other sick children popped into his head and the tension in his body eased. There were many children suffering from incurable illnesses, and they didn't have parents who were researchers in the most powerful pharmaceutical company in the world to help them.

He could be of service. He thrust the thought away quickly so his DNA couldn't read it. He was still irritated by what they had told him. It was too much for one person to absorb all at once.

"We must go now. Before we do, we want you to remember this." The dragons aligned themselves vertically in front of him like soldiers. "DNA is the mastermind of your body, your soul. But DNA has a master as well." The twelve dragons spun and fused themselves into two mighty golden dragons. "That master is you. *YOU* are the master to mastermind."

Nathan stared at the DNA-dragons with glittering scales and long whiskers. *The master is you.* He absorbed those words and their meaning. The power was within him.

"Where are you going?" he asked.

"Here and there. You have more power than you realize. Use that power wisely. Use it responsibly."

With that, the golden dragons faded, leaving him alone in the lab to consider everything that had just happened.

***

The next morning, Nathan held his wife's hand as they headed to Lisa Matthews's presentation. Lisa had just returned from her travels in Asia and Australia and was presenting her new discoveries to the research team. She always brought back unique findings that could assist the company with innovative endeavors in health, beauty, and technology.

"How are you feeling?" Heather asked, searching his eyes for any signs of fatigue.

He held up his large cup of blue bean coffee and smiled. "Fine. Don't worry, honey, I'm all right."

Last night, Nathan had told his wife everything. Though she had listened, she took the extra precaution of monitoring his temperature and examining him thoroughly. She insisted on confirming he was himself because he had sounded like a man who had lost his mind. She feared he had ingested some toxic fumes and had come home belligerent, talking foolish things. After he proved that he was sane by giving her private details of their first date, she finally calmed down enough to concentrate on his bloodwork. There had been no sign of infection or unknown diseases lurking in his blood. The scars he had acquired in the portal had all disappeared.

Even though Heather was an open-minded and brilliant scientist, he could tell she didn't believe his story. What normal person would, without proof? No one would fully believe in the phenomenon if they hadn't experienced it themselves.

He gave her the space she needed to absorb it just as he had needed time to come to terms with communicating with his own DNA. He hadn't seen or heard from it, or rather, them, since last night. Perhaps their physical visit had been a one-time thing, and future communication would be more subtle, like the tingle or the innate knowing he felt whenever he thought of them or talked to them in his mind.

He admitted he had been given a gift. He acknowledged and respected it, promising he'd use it in a beneficial way.

Right now, his first priority was Rena. He had a list of theories he wanted to experiment with right after this presentation.

Lisa entered the conference room, nodded to the audience, and walked to the podium. She pulled out three virtual screens that splashed across the room, each one displaying images of plants, insects, and an orange and black bird.

"Thank you for coming today. I'm excited to show you these specimens." Lisa's eyes beamed with excitement. "Here are a few plants with healing properties. This curly leaf one can block out ultraviolet light better than any sunblock we currently have."

Nathan studied the plants and insects that Lisa described. Their department could definitely benefit from these new findings.

Then the two screens went away, leaving the one with the bird. Lisa expanded the screen so he could see details. It looked like a sparrow, but just orange and black.

"This rare bird is the Hooded Pitohui, the most poisonous bird on the planet. It's from New Guinea." Lisa went on to describe the village where she found it, but Nathan didn't hear any of it.

All Nathan heard was that it was the most poisonous bird on the planet. Excitement roared through his blood as if that statement had been the activation he'd been waiting for. That same powerful feeling of inner knowing he had felt inside the portal reemerged. He trusted the feeling and knew exactly what he had to do.

He gripped Heather's hand and squeezed hard. She glanced over and met his eyes, trying to read them. He mouthed, "Later."

Without a doubt, he knew this bird was the catalyst that would bring his speculation to the next level. Based on what he had experienced with the mutant coronavirus and the cancerous grub, he pondered exploring poison with poison. He had felt how the two had interacted inside his body. Perhaps the cure to a potent poison was to use another poison. He was curious to see what this bird would do to Rena's illness.

After the conference, Nathan headed toward Lisa's office to discuss an innovative collaboration. He needed a specimen of that bird.

"What's the gleam in your eyes?" Heather asked.

"We're going to heal Rena. That bird is her hope."

A tingle brushed across his shoulder and Nathan knew that his DNA had just sent him the confirmation he needed.

Acknowledgements

Good people are the true magic in this world. I am fortunate to have them around me. I'm truly grateful for Anna Nesbitt, Laurie Bell, Carolyn Vaughan, and so many other amazing writers. You understand the power of words and stories, and you have all helped me make this story better. With all my heart, thank you.

Finally, thank you to my husband, Jonathan, for his love, endless support, and patience. It takes exemplary skills to maneuver safely around me when I'm working on many projects, and he has those admirable skills. Thank you for holding space for me to be creative. And thank you to my children who cheer me on even when they don't fully understand the magnitude of their support.

ABOUT THE AUTHOR

Linh Nguyen-Ng

Pronounced: Lynn — New Yen — Ing

I love the arts, words, colors, texture, and esoteric thinking. I dwell in the multiverse, including the magical world of children's books. I live in Massachusetts with my husband and two creative children. The four seasons inspire me with their changing beauty.

I'd love to hear from you. Connect with me with below!

www.linhnguyenng.com
Instagram: @landscaper.of.words
Facebook: www.facebook.com/lnguyenng/
Twitter: @linhnguyenng
https://www.pinterest.com/linhnguyenng/

www.ingramcontent.com/pod-product-compliance
Lightning Source LLC
Chambersburg PA
CBHW070944120726
47908CB00005BA/1511